North Dakota

Minnesota

South Dakota

Wisconsin

Michigan

New York

Massachusetts

Rhode Island

Connecticut

Nebraska

Iowa

Pennsylvania

New Jersey

Illinois

Indiana

Ohio

Delaware

Maryland

Kansas

Missouri

West Virginia

Virginia

Washington, D.C.

Kentucky

North Carolina

Oklahoma

Arkansas

Tennessee

South Carolina

Texas

Mississippi

Alabama

Georgia

Louisiana

Florida

COLORADO

KANSAS

MISSOURI

ARKANSAS

NEW MEXICO

TEXAS

• Beaver

Waynoka

Little Sahara
State Park

Woodward

Enid

Pawhuska

Tall Grass
Prarie Reserve

Tulsa

Catoosa

Stillwater

Arkansas River

Guthrie

Edmond

Arcadia

Chandler

Eufaula Lake

Canadian River

★ OKLAHOMA CITY

Moore

Wetumka

Norman

Anadarko

Chickasha

Lawton

Wilburton

Robbers
Cave State
Park

Lake Texona

Red River

For Etha

The Twelve Days of Christmas in Oklahoma

written by
Tammi Sauer

illustrated by
Victoria Hutto

STERLING CHILDREN'S BOOKS
New York

Dear Addison,

Are you ready for rodeos, road trips, and more? I hope so because Mom, Dad, and I have a <u>lot</u> planned for you to see and do during your visit to Oklahoma. I wish I could give you every detail in this letter, but I want your stay to be full of surprises.

I will tell you three things:

1. Don't forget to pack a coat. It's usually cold here in the winter, but Oklahoma's weather can be a little crazy. Yesterday it was 35 degrees. Tomorrow it's supposed to be 62!

2. Come hungry! Mom and Dad plan to make Oklahoma's state meal while you're here. This includes fried okra, squash, cornbread, barbecue pork, biscuits, sausage and gravy, grits, corn, chicken fried steak, black-eyed peas, <u>and</u> pecan pie.

3. Be ready for **ANYTHING**—even a helicopter ride or two courtesy of my dad! We want you to see as much of Oklahoma as possible. ☺

Can't wait for you to get here. Having you with us will make this our best Christmas ever!

Your cousin and soon-to-be Oklahoma tour guide,

Ethan

Dear Mom and Dad,

My trip to Oklahoma is off to a great start! As soon as Uncle Jack, Aunt Jen, and Ethan picked me up from the airport, we headed straight for the Chickasha Festival of Light. We went on a carriage ride, drank hot chocolate, ate gooey cinnamon rolls, and soaked up 43 acres of twinkling scenery.

I loved the displays and decorated trees, but my favorite part was walking down the crystal pedestrian bridge. I was surrounded by 75,000 lights at once!

Just as we were about to leave, Ethan pointed out a scissor-tailed flycatcher (Oklahoma's state bird)! He was right next to us, perched on the branch of a redbud tree (Oklahoma's state tree). I even gave him a name. Snip! When Snip took flight, his tail really did open up like a pair of scissors. How cool is that?

Hugs and kisses from Oklahoma,

Addison

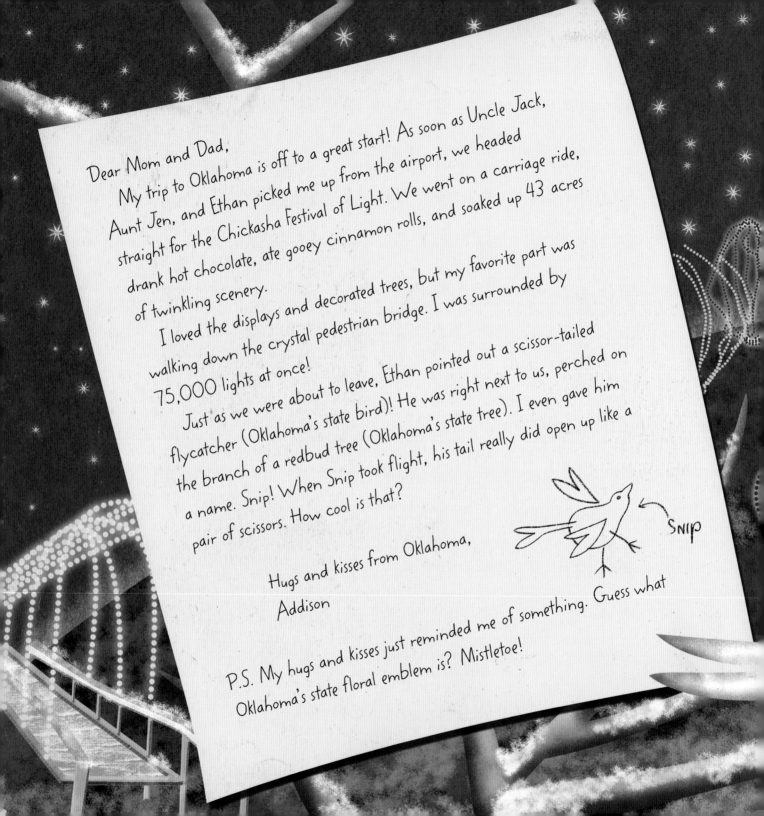

SNIP

P.S. My hugs and kisses just reminded me of something. Guess what Oklahoma's state floral emblem is? Mistletoe!

On the first day of Christmas,
my cousin gave to me . . .

a flycatcher in a redbud tree.

Howdy, partners!

Oklahoma is BIG on cowboys. I saw the proof at the National Cowboy & Western Heritage Museum in Oklahoma City. It's the West at its best!

After the museum, we went to a real live rodeo. It was held at Guthrie's Lazy E Arena, which is the largest indoor rodeo arena in the world. I loved watching the barrel racing and steer wrestling, but the bull riding was my favorite event. Yeehaw!

Ethan told me that Oklahoma once had Wild West Shows, too. These shows were jam-packed with action, trick performances, and theatrical reenactments. Zack Mulhall, a rancher outside of Guthrie, started his own show called the Congress of Rough Riders and Ropers. His daughter Lucille was one of the stars and is celebrated as America's first cowgirl. Not only could Lucille ride and rope, but she taught her horse to do nearly 40 tricks. She even trained him how to take off a man's coat and put it back on again! Will Rogers often performed in this show, too. His skills and sense of humor made him one of the most popular people of his time.

All in all, today was a rip-roarin' wild ride.

Your little buckaroo,
Addison

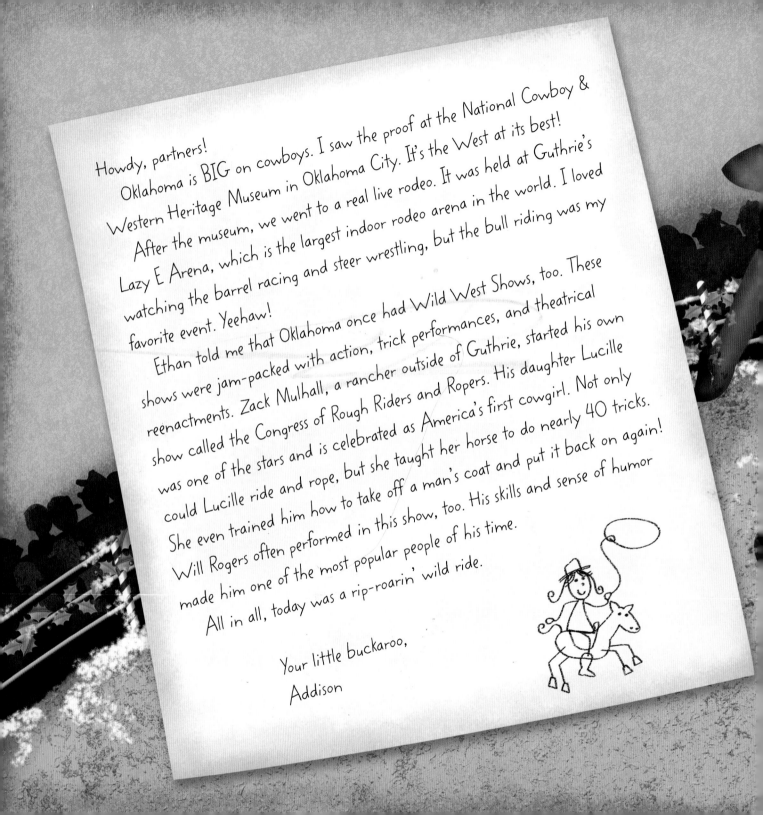

On the second day of Christmas,
my cousin gave to me . . .

2 bucking bulls

and a flycatcher in a redbud tree.

Dear Mom and Dad,

Newsflash: penguins have invaded the city of Tulsa, Oklahoma! Aunt Jen told me that when the Tulsa Zoo wanted to add an African black-footed penguin exhibit, it held a fundraiser like no other. Businesses gave big donations. In exchange, each one got a very special delivery— a six-foot-tall painted penguin sculpture!

Ethan and I spotted more than a dozen penguins on our hunt today. I think Snip enjoyed them as much as we did! My favorites were the polka-dotted penguin, the policeman penguin, and the oh-so-graceful ballerina penguin. Best of all, we even visited the REAL penguins at the zoo!

There's more to Tulsa than penguins, though. Ethan said that during the 1920s oil boom, Tulsa was rich, rich, rich! A lot of that money went into creating some really fancy buildings in a cool style called "Art Deco." As we walked up and down the streets, I almost felt like I was in a fairy tale.

Oohing and aahing
in Oklahoma,
Addison

elephant

LION

On the third day of Christmas,
my cousin gave to me . . .

3 penguins

2 bucking bulls,
and a flycatcher in a redbud tree.

Dear Mom and Dad,

We spent the day in Stillwater, home of Red Dirt Music. This music got its name from the iron-rich red soil found in Oklahoma, and it has a style that's different from anything I've ever heard before. Mix together some country, folk, blues, western swing, and rock, and you have Red Dirt Music. Consider me a fan!

We had lunch at a fun place called Eskimo Joe's. Burgers and cheese fries. YUM! After that, we headed to the Town & Gown Theatre. We saw a great play and even went on a backstage tour. I loved seeing the set design area and the costume shop. Want to know the best part? Our tour guide told us that some people are convinced the theatre is haunted! Sometimes strange footsteps can be heard. Doors mysteriously open and shut. People say they've even heard their names being called when no one else is around. Doesn't that sound spooktacular?

Your boo-tiful daughter,
Addison

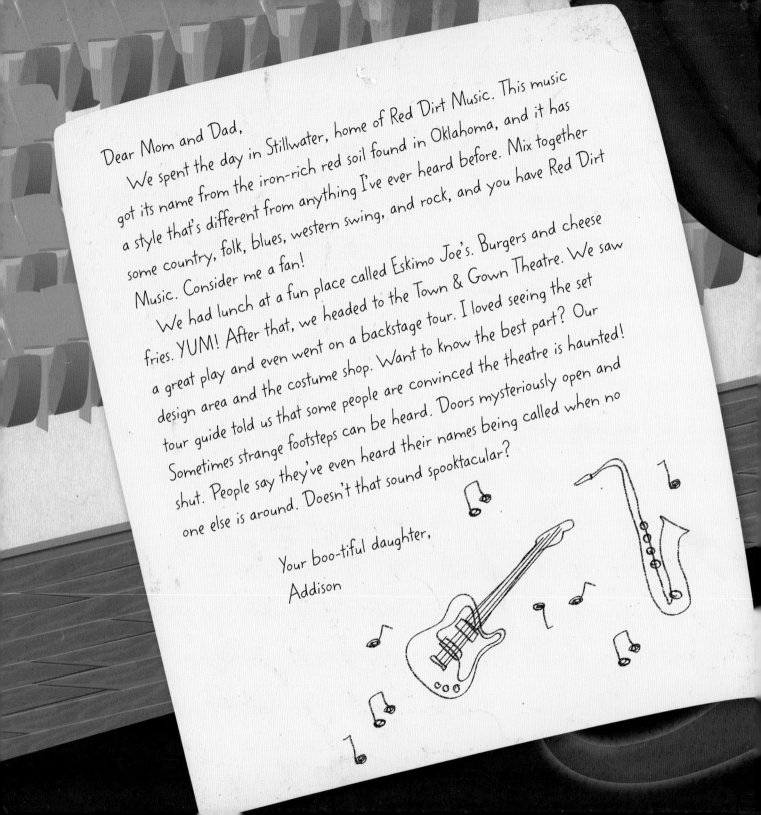

On the fourth day of Christmas,
my cousin gave to me . . .

4 spooky ghosts

3 penguins, 2 bucking bulls,
and a flycatcher in a redbud tree.

Dear Mom and Dad,

Today was filled with wild rides. Wild ride number one—we hit the sky in a helicopter courtesy of Uncle Jack. It was so much fun! I NEED to get a pilot's license as soon as I'm old enough.

Wild ride number two took place after we landed. This time Aunt Jen was in charge. Hello, dune buggies!

The four of us strapped on helmets and went for a ride at Little Sahara State Park near the town of Waynoka. Aunt Jen took us up and around the smaller dunes, but we saw some dunes that were seventy-five feet high! The fine quartz sand at Little Sahara covers over 1,600 acres. It was like being in one giant, hilly sandbox.

Ethan said Little Sahara State Park is just one of dozens of state parks in Oklahoma, filled with everything from lakes to forests to mountains. A couple of them even have giant waterfalls! Ethan's favorite park is near Wilburton. It's called Robbers Cave State Park. Legend has it that famous outlaws like Jesse James, Belle Starr, and the Dalton Gang used Robbers Cave as one of their hideouts from the law.

From dunes to desperados,
Addison

REWARD
$750.00
Belle Starr

WANTED
JESSE JAMES

On the fifth day of Christmas,
my cousin gave to me . . .

5 golden dunes

4 spooky ghosts, 3 penguins, 2 bucking bulls,
and a flycatcher in a redbud tree.

Dear Mom and Dad,

Today Uncle Jack and Aunt Jen took us on a road trip down Route 66. In case you didn't know, Route 66 is a highway that was built in 1926 to connect Chicago and Los Angeles. It has a couple of nicknames, too. Some people call it "The Main Street of America." Other people call it "The Mother Road." Me? I call it <u>awesome!</u>

Our adventures began with lunch at Pops in Arcadia. This restaurant is amazing. It offers nearly 600 kinds of ice-cold sodas, plus it has a 65-foot-tall neon bottle of pop towering outside the building! I had a Zuberfizz Grape Soda and Ethan had one of the 65 kinds of root beer. Mmm-mmm good.

A little ways down the road, we saw another Route 66 landmark—the Round Barn. We HAD to check it out! This barn is over 100 years old. It once held livestock. It even held town dances. Now it holds a special spot in Oklahoma's history. Some people love this Route 66 attraction so much, they've even gotten married there.

Our next stop was Catoosa. Ethan promised that if I kept my eyes open, I might spot a blue whale. Guess what? He was right! Just outside my window was a smiley 80-foot-long whale that was built out of pipe and concrete. As soon as Uncle Jack stopped the car, Ethan and I jumped out and raced straight inside the whale's mouth.

When we finally headed for home, Uncle Jack sang show tunes. Of course, "Oklahoma!" was our favorite. Even Snip sang along.

One thing's for sure. I got my kicks on Route 66.

Vroom-vroom,
Addison

On the sixth day of Christmas, my cousin gave to me . . .

6 cars a-zooming

5 golden dunes, 4 spooky ghosts, 3 penguins,
2 bucking bulls, and a flycatcher in a redbud tree.

Dear Mom and Dad,

Did you know Oklahoma has one of the largest American Indian populations of any state? The name Oklahoma comes from two Choctaw words: "Okla" meaning red and "homa" meaning people. Symbols from the Cherokee, Choctaw, Creek, Chickasaw, and Seminole Nations can even be found on the state seal.

Today we went to Anadarko and visited the Indian City USA Cultural Center. My favorite part was getting to see the reconstructed dwellings of the Navaho, Wichita, Kiowa Winter Camp, Caddo, Pawnee, Pueblo, and Chiricahua Apache. Tribal members and anthropologists helped to make the various villages look authentic. I felt like I was stepping back in time.

Ethan says I need to come back to Oklahoma in the summer for the Red Earth Native American Cultural Festival. Over a thousand American Indian artists and dancers gather each year to practice ancient customs and celebrate their heritage. I would love to see the artwork and traditional clothing, but I think I'd be most excited to watch the dance competitions. I bet they're amazing!

Chi pisa lachike.
(That means "I'll see you soon" in Choctaw.)
Addison

On the seventh day of Christmas, my cousin gave to me . . .

7 handmade treasures

6 cars a-zooming, 5 golden dunes,
4 spooky ghosts, 3 penguins, 2 bucking bulls,
and a flycatcher in a redbud tree.

On your mark. Get set. Go!

At noon on April 22, 1889, gunshots fired, cannons blasted, and bugles sounded across Oklahoma. Fifty thousand people took off on foot, horseback, and covered wagon. I had one question for Ethan: WHY? He told me that President Benjamin Harrison had just declared two million acres of land open for settlement, and everyone wanted a piece of it. This Land Run was one of the biggest events in Oklahoma history.

Uncle Jack took us to see the Centennial Land Run Monument in downtown Oklahoma City. I could almost hear the thundering horses and taste the clouds of dust. It was easy to imagine the determination of those pioneers who raced to stake their claims and start a new life. Ethan's school reenacts the Land Run each spring. Once I heard that, I decided WE needed to have one of our own. We each grabbed a stick and took off to claim plots of land.

Thanks to Ethan, I learned some crazy facts about the Land Run.

Fact One: Some people cheated! They entered the race early so they could claim the best plots of land. They became known as Sooners because they arrived too soon.

Fact Two: Guthrie, Oklahoma, went from having a few residents that morning to having 10,000 by afternoon. Oklahomans joke that Rome wasn't built in a day, but Guthrie sure was!

Staking a claim in Oklahoma,

Addison

On the eighth day of Christmas, my cousin gave to me . . .

8 horses racing

7 handmade treasures, 6 cars a-zooming, 5 golden dunes,
4 spooky ghosts, 3 penguins, 2 bucking bulls,
and a flycatcher in a redbud tree.

Dear Mom and Dad,

Did you ever notice that the state of Oklahoma is kinda shaped like a pan? Well, today Uncle Jack flew us to the Oklahoma Panhandle (that's what this part of the state is actually called!), and we visited the town of Beaver. Back in 1879, this town was a fur-trading post. Now it has a different claim to fame. Beaver is known as the Cow Chip Throwing Capital of the World. Ha! (In case you didn't know, a cow chip is a dried-up pile of cow poop!) Each spring, people come from all over to participate in the World Championship Cow Chip Throw.

These are the rules:

* The chip must be at least six inches in diameter.
 * The chip has to be picked from the official dung truck.
  * The chip cannot be tampered with in any way.
   * If the chip breaks in flight, the piece that goes the farthest gets counted.

Ethan hopes to enter the big event, so we did what we had to do—we practiced! Lucky for Uncle Jack, he managed to duck just in time! And lucky for us, cow chips were easy to find. Ethan says almost three-fourths of Oklahoma's land is used for cattle grazing and growing crops like winter wheat, hay, corn, peanuts, and pecans.

Later, when we stopped at a roadside diner for a snack, I told Ethan I prefer Oklahoma's pecan pies to its cow pies any day! I also love Oklahoma's apple pies and cherry crumb pies and pumpkin pies and . . . well, you get the idea.

Love and cow chips,
Addison

COW CHIP

COUSIN ETHAN

On the ninth day of Christmas, my cousin gave to me . . .

9 pies a-steaming

8 horses racing, 7 handmade treasures, 6 cars a-zooming,
5 golden dunes, 4 spooky ghosts, 3 penguins, 2 bucking bulls,
and a flycatcher in a redbud tree.

Dear Mom and Dad,

Today we toured the National Weather Center in Norman. I found out just how tough Oklahomans can be. Did you know that in May 1999, one of the worst tornadoes in history struck Moore, Oklahoma? The path of destruction was nearly a mile wide! It tossed cars into the sky, left a school in shambles, and destroyed hundreds and hundreds of homes.

That wasn't the only twister to hit this state. Oklahoma is in Tornado Alley. This means it gets <u>lots</u> of tornadoes.

When conditions are right, a tornado watch is issued. If a tornado is actually spotted, a tornado warning is given. Sirens sound and meteorologists urge people to <u>take shelter immediately</u>. Ethan said his family heads straight for their underground storm shelter. They keep water, flashlights, batteries, a first-aid kit, and a radio in it at all times.

And at Ethan's school, they don't just have fire drills, they have tornado drills, too! This helps kids and teachers to know exactly what to do and where to go in case a tornado heads their way.

This has definitely been a whirlwind of a trip so far!

Your little tornado,
Addison

Tornado Alley

On the tenth day of Christmas, my cousin gave to me . . .

10 twisters twisting

9 pies a-steaming, **8** horses racing,
7 handmade treasures, **6** cars a-zooming, **5** golden dunes,
4 spooky ghosts, **3** penguins, **2** bucking bulls,
and a flycatcher in a redbud tree.

Dear Mom and Dad,

What weighs almost a ton, runs faster than 30 miles per hour, and is brown all over?

Bison!

Uncle Jack said no trip to Oklahoma would be complete without seeing the state animal in the wild, so he took us for a drive through the Tall Grass Prairie Reserve near Pawhuska. We saw white-tailed deer, coyotes, and—just as we had hoped—bison!

They were HUGE. I loved their short horns and shaggy winter coats. I wanted to pet one, but Ethan said that was a terrible idea. Bison may look peaceful, but they can be very feisty.

Oh, and I've GOT to come back to Oklahoma next summer. That's when the state flying mammal—the Mexican free-tailed bat—comes to Oklahoma to breed. We could be part of a bat watch at Selman Bat Cave near Woodward. As the sun sets, more than a _million_ bats whoosh from the cave and into the sky. They have one thing on their minds—dinner! These bats eat <u>ten tons</u> of mosquitoes, moths, and beetles each night. And you thought <u>I</u> was a big eater.

Your not-so-batty daughter,
Addison

On the eleventh day of Christmas, my cousin gave to me . . .

11 bison grazing

10 twisters twisting, **9** pies a-steaming, **8** horses racing,
7 handmade treasures, **6** cars a-zooming, **5** golden dunes,
4 spooky ghosts, **3** penguins, **2** bucking bulls,
and a flycatcher in a redbud tree.

Dear Mom and Dad,

Oklahoma has a <u>great</u> sense of humor.

Today we went to Wetumka, and I learned about something that happened back in the summer of 1950. A sweet-talking man named F. Bam Morrison persuaded the local residents to put up money to bring a circus to town. The whole town made preparations, and the hotel and café even gave Morrison free room and board. Everyone was so excited. A circus was coming!

Well, the big day arrived, but guess what? No circus! F. Bam Morrison had tricked the townspeople and snuck off with their money the night before! At first, everybody felt terrible. Then they laughed at themselves and decided to hold a celebration anyway.

Nearly every September since, Wetumka has held a Sucker Day Festival. It's a time for everyone to laugh over the day they were conned and have some serious fun. Bands play. Sometimes there are rodeos and talent shows. There's even a parade.

Ethan and I were wishing we could be a part of it all when something amazing happened. The people of Wetumka invited us to join their nighttime Christmas Parade! It was so cool. Floats with lights. Awesome music. And you will never believe the best part of all . . . Santa and Mrs. Claus showed up on Harleys! Ha! They even let Ethan and me catch a ride. Of course, Snip joined in on the fun, too.

When you pick me up at the airport tomorrow, do you think you could bring a truck? I have a few gifts to bring home. . . .

Missing Oklahoma already,
Addison

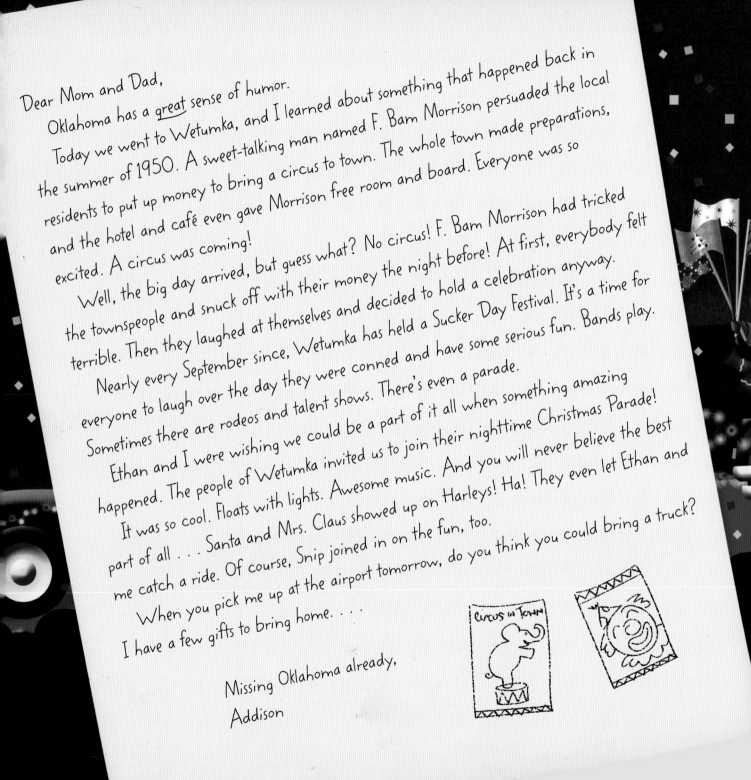

On the twelfth day of Christmas, my cousin gave to me . . .

12 flags a-waving

11 bison grazing, **10** twisters twisting, **9** pies a-steaming,
8 horses racing, **7** handmade treasures, **6** cars a-zooming,
5 golden dunes, **4** spooky ghosts, **3** penguins, **2** bucking bulls,
and a flycatcher in a redbud tree.

OKLAHOMA, where the wind comes sweepin' down the plain...

JOY

NOEL

Get Your
on Route

Oklahoma: The Sooner State

Capital: Oklahoma City • **State bird:** the scissor-tailed flycatcher • **State animal:** the bison • **State flying mammal:** the Mexican free-tailed bat • **State reptile:** the collared lizard • **State amphibian:** the bullfrog • **State insect:** the honeybee • **State flower:** the Oklahoma rose • **State tree:** the redbud • **State rock:** rose rock • **State beverage:** milk • **State song:** "Oklahoma!" • **State folk dance:** the square dance • **State motto:** "Labor Conquers All Things"

Some Famous Oklahomans:

Garth Brooks (1962–) was born in Tulsa and grew up in Yukon. This award-winning singer-songwriter is a key figure in the history of country music who is best known for his number-one hits such as "If Tomorrow Never Comes" and "The Thunder Rolls." In 1996, he was inducted into the Country Music Hall of Fame.

Kristin Chenoweth (1968–) was born in Broken Arrow and is a singer as well as a stage, screen, and television actress. She is best known on Broadway for her Tony-winning performance in *You're a Good Man, Charlie Brown* and for originating the role of Glinda the Good Witch in the musical *Wicked*.

Mickey Mantle (1931–1995) was born in Spavinaw. "The Mick" won four home-run championships, a Triple Crown, and three Most Valuable Player (MVP) awards during his eighteen-year career with the New York Yankees. He is considered one of the greatest baseball players of all time.

Reba McEntire (1955–) was born in McAlester and is a country music singer as well as an actress. She began her solo career after getting discovered during her performance of the national anthem at the National Rodeo Finals in Oklahoma City. Since then she has scored more than thirty number-one hits, numerous awards, and a star on the Hollywood Walk of Fame.

Shannon Miller (1977–) grew up in Edmond and is a seven-time Olympic Medalist. She is celebrated as America's most decorated female gymnast. A bronze statue of Miller is located in Edmond's Shannon Miller Park.

Wiley Post (1898–1935) lived in various parts of Oklahoma, including Mayville. He was a pioneer in aviation and the first person to fly solo around the world.

Will Rogers (1879–1935) was born near present-day Oologah. He was a cowboy, social commenter, humorist, vaudeville performer, and actor. He is known as Oklahoma's favorite son.

To every kid in Oklahoma. —T.S.

To my wonderful, talented husband, Ralph.
Thank you for your constant support and encouragement in all that I choose to do. —V.Y.H.

STERLING CHILDREN'S BOOKS
New York

An Imprint of Sterling Publishing
387 Park Avenue South
New York, NY 10016

STERLING CHILDREN'S BOOKS and the distinctive Sterling Children's Books logo are trademarks
of Sterling Publishing Co., Inc.

Text © 2012 by Tammi Sauer
Illustrations © 2012 by Victoria Hutto
The illustrations for this book were created digitally.
Designed by Elizabeth Phillips.

ISBN 978-1-4027-9224-3

Library of Congress Cataloging-in-Publication Data

Sauer, Tammi.
    The twelve days of Christmas in Oklahoma / written by Tammi Sauer ; illustrated by Victoria Hutto.
        p. cm.
    Summary: Addison writes a letter home each of the twelve days she spends exploring the state of Oklahoma at
Christmastime, as her cousin Ethan shows her everything from the Chickasha Festival of Light to a cow chip throw.
Includes facts about Oklahoma.
    ISBN 978-1-4027-9224-3
    [1. Oklahoma--Fiction. 2. Christmas--Fiction. 3. Cousins--Fiction. 4. Letters--Fiction.] I. Hutto, Victoria, ill. II. Title.
PZ7.S2502Twe 2012
[Fic]--dc23
                                                      2011040850

Distributed in Canada by Sterling Publishing
c/o Canadian Manda Group, 165 Dufferin Street
Toronto, Ontario, Canada M6K 3H6
Distributed in the United Kingdom by GMC Distribution Services
Castle Place, 166 High Street, Lewes, East Sussex, England BN7 1XU
Distributed in Australia by Capricorn Link (Australia) Pty. Ltd.
P.O. Box 704, Windsor, NSW 2756, Australia

For information about custom editions, special sales, and premium and corporate purchases,
please contact Sterling Special Sales at 800-805-5489 or specialsales@sterlingpublishing.com.

Printed in China

Lot #:
2 4 6 8 10 9 7 5 3 1
07/12

www.sterlingpublishing.com/kids

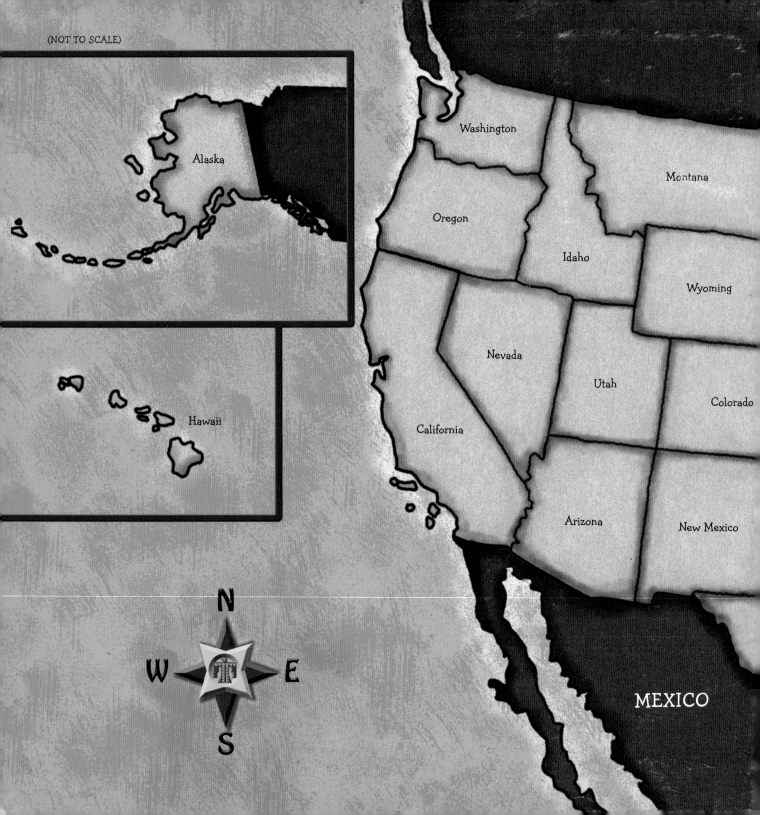

(NOT TO SCALE)

Alaska

Hawaii

Washington

Oregon

Idaho

Montana

Wyoming

Nevada

Utah

Colorado

California

Arizona

New Mexico

MEXICO

N

W   E

S